T0402422

Crisis

Teen Mental Health at Risk

Leanne Currie-McGhee

San Diego, CA

© 2024 ReferencePoint Press, Inc.
Printed in the United States

For more information, contact:
ReferencePoint Press, Inc.
PO Box 27779
San Diego, CA 92198
www.ReferencePointPress.com

LIBRARY OF CONGRESS CATALOGING-IN-PUBLICATION DATA

Names: Currie-McGhee, Leanne author.
Title: Crisis: Teen Mental Health at Risk/ Leanne Currie-McGhee.
Description: San Diego, CA : ReferencePoint Press, Inc., 2024. | Includes
  bibliographical references and index.
Identifiers: LCCN 2023019413 (print) | ISBN
  9781678205645 (library binding) | ISBN 9781678205652 (ebook)
Subjects: LCSH: Mental health--Juvenile literature.

CONTENTS

Emerging Crisis

At age thirteen, a suburban Minneapolis girl (identified for privacy reasons as M) started cutting. At the time, M was attending virtual school due to the COVID-19 pandemic. Even before the pandemic, M had been experiencing anxiety. But once virtual school began, the lack of interaction with others, the pressure of independently keeping up with schoolwork, and the hours spent on social media led to an increase in M's negative feelings. One evening, M went upstairs, found scissors, and cut both ankles. "I was mad at myself for not doing homework," M said. "I was kind of thinking, 'Oh, the pain feels good,' like it was better than being stressed."[1]

M is just one example of millions of teens dealing with mental health issues. Many of these young people have experienced extreme loneliness during lockdowns, peer pressure and cyberbullying on social media, and a variety of vulnerabilities based on race, ethnicity, or gender identity. According to mental health professionals, all of this has contributed to a growing number of youth who are struggling. The problem is so great that in the fall of 2021 the American Academy of Pediatrics, along with the American Academy of Child & Adolescent Psychiatry and the Children's Hospital Association, declared a national emergency in child and adolescent mental health. Many factors led to this declaration, in particular that rates of youth mental health issues, emergency room visits due to mental health, and suicide rose steadily from 2010 to 2020.

COVID-19 Effects

Since the declaration, the crisis among youth has only gotten worse. The statistics show increasing mental health issues among teens. In 2023 the Centers for Disease Control and Prevention (CDC) released its annual Youth Risk Behavior Survey that provided information on youth mental health through 2021. The survey revealed that 42 percent of the seventeen thousand teens surveyed felt persistently sad or hopeless in 2021, compared to 28 percent in 2011 and 37 percent in 2019. Other indicators of declining mental health, such as suicide attempts, also rose in the same time period.

The COVID-19 pandemic is believed to have exacerbated an already serious problem among youth. During the first year of the pandemic, many teens attended virtual classes from their homes because schools closed in-person classes. Teens' sports and social activities were curtailed, and they did not see their peers nor interact with supportive adults such as coaches and teachers. As a result, many teens experienced social isolation. For many, this led to increased loneliness and instability. This occurred not just in the United States but worldwide. An analysis of twenty-nine youth mental health studies around the world with over eighty thousand global participants, published in the summer of 2021 in *JAMA Pediatrics*, found that depression and anxiety in youth doubled compared to pre-pandemic levels. "We know children benefit from stability, structure, routine and the support of trusting adults, but during the pandemic, we've seen an increase in overall instability and changing structures," says pediatric psychologist Ethan Benore. "Now, we're seeing an increased volume of children needing a higher level of care."[2]

Kaylie Rosen was among those young people who struggled during the pandemic. The lockdown took away many of her coping methods for dealing with

> "We know children benefit from stability, structure, routine and the support of trusting adults, but during the pandemic, we've seen an increase in overall instability and changing structures."[2]
>
> —Ethan Benore, pediatric psychologist

anxiety and obsessive-compulsive disorder (OCD), which she had developed in the fourth grade. By age seventeen, she had received treatment and was thriving at boarding school, using the tools she had learned in therapy. A major coping skill was relying on strong relationships with friends when feeling low. Then the pandemic hit, and she and all her friends were sent home from boarding school. "I don't do well at home," Rosen says. "My friends mean the world to me. They get me through everything. The fact that I can't see them, which is the way I usually deal with my life, was devastating."[3]

During the time at home, Rosen struggled but found ways to care for her mental health. Art therapy helped her deal with anxious thoughts. Interacting with others through teaching online English classes to kids in Africa helped alleviate her loneliness. After boarding school reopened her senior year, Rosen attended and graduated, going on to Tulane University in Louisiana.

Why This Must Be Addressed

Rosen was able to care for her mental health because, through previous counseling and therapy, she had gained an understanding of her health issues and learned ways to handle them. Without this, she could have spiraled into a path of increased depression and possibly self-harm. This is why professionals are calling attention to the mental health crisis among youth. They believe the need for interventions now is great. Many have urged schools to provide mental health services. They have also called for greater access to mental health providers.

If the current trend continues, and if mental health issues are not addressed among the nation's young people, the results could be disastrous. Of the teens who took part in the 2023 Youth Risk Behavior Survey, nearly a quarter (22 percent) said they had seri-

Mental Health Among Teens Worsens

US teens are increasingly experiencing feelings of sadness and hopelessness and are thinking about suicide more now than in the past. This is the finding of a survey conducted by the Centers for Disease Control and Prevention and published in February 2023. The survey is done every two years among a nationally representative sampling of students in public and private high schools. The survey shows progressively worsening mental health among teens between 2011 and 2021.

The percentage of high school students who:	2011 Total	2013 Total	2015 Total	2017 Total	2019 Total	2021 Total
Experienced persistent feelings of sadness or hopelessness	28%	30%	30%	31%	37%	42%
Experienced poor mental health	–	–	–	–	–	29%
Seriously considered attempting suicide	16%	17%	18%	17%	19%	22%
Made a suicide plan	13%	14%	15%	14%	16%	18%
Attempted suicide	8%	8%	9%	7%	9%	10%
Were injured in a suicide attempt that had to be treated by a doctor or nurse	2%	3%	3%	2%	3%	3%

Source: Centers for Disease Control and Prevention, "Youth Risk Behavior Survey Data Summary & Trends Report 2009–2019," 2020. www.cdc.gov.

ously considered suicide. This contrasts with 19 percent in 2019 and 16 percent in 2011. Self-harm, suicide, and hospitalizations due to mental health issues are continuing to rise, and without addressing the crisis, the likelihood is that these serious results of mental health problems will increase.

As happened with M, depression and anxiety led to more cutting and to suicidal thoughts. M's parents have been very involved, ensuring that their daughter has received proper treatment, medication, and therapy. It has not been an easy road, but their efforts continue.

CHAPTER ONE

Teens in Distress

Madison Jo Sieminski knew in high school that something was wrong with how she felt. "Since sophomore year of high school, I noticed I was never fully myself," writes Sieminski. "There has been someone inside of my head telling me to constantly worry and hold back from everything. Did I listen? Of course, I did. I withdrew and shrank into myself until January 1st, 2020, when I sought help. Up until then, I had failed to realize my mental health was important and I needed help."[4] Sieminski was diagnosed with severe anxiety and depression, and when she sought help, she was able to get treated. She is one of many youth who have dealt with a mental health issue.

Mental health disorders are becoming increasingly common among teens today. "Three decades ago, the gravest public health threats to teenagers in the United States came from binge drinking, drunken driving, teenage pregnancy, and smoking. These have since fallen sharply, replaced by a new public health concern: soaring rates of mental health disorders,"[5] writes *New York Times* reporter Matt Richtel. Richtel spent more than a year interviewing adolescents and their families for a series on the mental health crisis. Today the mental health disorders that teens grapple with the most are anxiety, depression, suicide, and self-harm, although these are not the only ones disrupting their lives.

Anxiety

Kyle Mitchell began experiencing anxiety as a child. His anxiety worsened in high school. He writes:

While I struggled with social anxiety even before adolescence, it was really in high school when it became apparent that it was beyond just being shy or socially awkward. I had always felt different and as early as kindergarten, I knew I behaved and thought differently. I had a hard time talking to people, making friends and any social event felt overwhelming and embarrassing, filling me with anxiety. But I just accepted it and didn't think I could do anything about it.[6]

It was not until college that Mitchell finally sought help, was diagnosed, and learned ways to manage his anxiety.

Mitchell is one of many youth who experience anxiety. According to the CDC, anxiety, behavioral problems, depression, and attention-deficit/hyperactivity disorder (ADHD) are the most commonly diagnosed mental disorders in children and teens. The CDC estimates that for youth aged three to seventeen years, during 2016 to 2019, approximately 9.4 percent were diagnosed with anxiety, 8.9 percent with behavioral problems, 4.4 percent with depression, and 9.8 percent with ADHD. Dealing with more than one of these conditions at a time is common, since, as the CDC notes, about three in four young people with depression also experience anxiety.

> "There has been someone inside of my head telling me to constantly worry and hold back from everything. Did I listen? Of course, I did. I withdrew and shrank into myself until January 1st, 2020, when I sought help."[4]
>
> —Madison Jo Sieminski, teenager who suffered from anxiety

Anxiety can come in different types—general anxiety, panic disorders, social anxiety, separation anxiety, and more. In all of them, the symptoms are similar no matter what triggers the reaction. These symptoms include experiencing feelings such as fear, uneasiness, panic, and agitation. Physical symptoms may manifest as nausea, shortness of breath, cold sweat, hyperventilation, insomnia, and more, with most people experiencing several symptoms at once. For many, these symptoms make it difficult

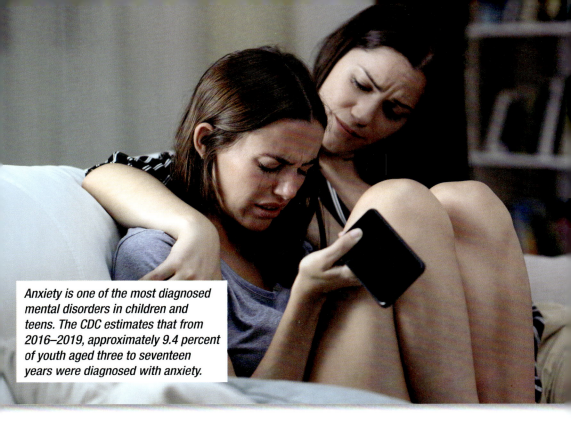

Anxiety is one of the most diagnosed mental disorders in children and teens. The CDC estimates that from 2016–2019, approximately 9.4 percent of youth aged three to seventeen years were diagnosed with anxiety.

to get through daily tasks and cause them to limit where they go and what they do.

Manvi Tiwari, who is from India, says she developed anxiety in her preteens and later developed OCD as well. Prior to the development of her symptoms, she had watched her mother go through depression and other mental health issues. Tiwari saw the positive effect treatment had on her mom but did not want to share what she herself was experiencing because she feared the stigma Indian society places on mental health problems. However, her anxiety and OCD intensified during the pandemic, and when she was seventeen, they began to severely disrupt her life. She decided to talk to her parents. "During the COVID-19 lockdown, I started to feel very anxious," Tiwari explains. "Often, I would cry and wouldn't even know the reason why I was crying. I told my parents that I want to opt for therapy."[7]

The therapy helped Tiwari get stronger, eventually leading her to becoming a mental health activist. Without her family's support and getting the help that was available, she is not sure what would have happened to her. "I still have OCD moments; I still get anxiety. I still seek help from professionals, but I am more or less cured," Tiwari explains. "My source of strength is my mother."[8] Overcoming the stigma associated with mental health, which is prevalent not just in India but in most countries, led to her finally getting help.

Depression Takes Its Toll

For some teens, battling depression is a daily part of their lives, causing many to feel despair and hopelessness. According to the National Institute of Mental Health, approximately 4.1 million US adolescents aged twelve to seventeen had at least one major depressive episode in 2020. This number represents 17 percent of US youth of this age range. During the same period, the percentage of young adults aged eighteen to twenty-five who experienced at least one major depressive episode was also 17 percent.

To be considered a depressive episode, according to the fifth edition of the *Diagnostic and Statistical Manual of Mental Disorders*, a person must experience at least two weeks of a depressed mood or be not interested in or take any pleasure from daily activities. Depression is usually accompanied by problems with sleeping, eating, energy, concentration, and self-worth. In severe cases it can lead to feelings and actions of self-harm and suicide. According to clinical psychologist Hanna Silva, a strong sign of depression is a feeling that nothing has meaning. To a person who is depressed, she says, "Most things are meaningless or hopeless. You feel that way even when positive things happen. For example, when your baby smiles at you, you can't feel joy."[9]

This was the case for Cora Berry, whose feelings about life grew darker from her preteen years until high school. Berry developed type 1 diabetes, a chronic condition in which the pancreas produces little or no insulin. Diabetes requires constant monitoring, lifelong treatment, and careful diet. When not properly managed, it can result in hospitalization. Because of this, by middle school she was missing a lot of school days. Those missed days added to her anxiety. She worried about not being able to keep up in school. By eighth grade, she started struggling with depression. She remembers not feeling like she fit in with friends or family and never feeling happiness.

It was in high school, as a freshman, that Berry's depression and anxiety worsened. She experienced a lot of stress trying to balance her classwork and other activities. She says:

> I hadn't told anyone what I was dealing with. . . . I was crying myself to sleep every night. I was really, really struggling with school, keeping up with it, because a lot of times I would be doing homework for like four hours after school, so I go to school for eight hours and I come home and I do like four hours of homework; on top of [that] I was in Orcasus, which was my school's dance company and I was dancing at my studio.[10]

When she started to feel like she wanted to self-harm, Berry finally opened up to her mother. This led to therapy and medication, which helped her manage the situation better and start on a road to recovery. After feeling stable for a few years, when she was seventeen, events that included dealing with kidney stones, her pet rabbit dying, and her parents separating led to another spiral into depression, and this time she felt like taking her own life. Because she told her parents about her feelings, she was able to get into a rehabilitation center, receive treatment, and learn coping skills anew. Back at home, she is moving forward in life and watching both her physical and mental health closely.

Self-Harm to Cope

Berry's depression led to thoughts of self-harm. She describes it as a coping skill, but a negative one. Berry, and other youth struggling with mental health, sometimes turn to self-harm to deal with their emotional pain. According to mental health professionals, it is a way to turn internal pain (which feels uncontrollable) into ex-

Studies and anecdotal evidence show that substance abuse in youth is tied to mental health disorders, one potentially leading to the other. The National Institutes of Health reports that over 60 percent of adolescents in community-based substance use disorder treatment programs are also dealing with a form of mental illness. When someone has two disorders or illnesses, it is called a comorbidity. Reasons for the comorbidity of substance abuse and mental health disorders vary, but they feed off of one another. Some youth with mental illnesses use alcohol or drugs to cope with the pain of their mental health issues. Other youth who are dealing with substance abuse develop anxiety and depression because of the issues this type of abuse brings to their lives. Whatever the cause, if a teen develops both problems, each can make the other disorder worse. And without treatment, teens' physical and emotional health can be in danger.

ternal pain (which feels somehow more manageable). In this way self-harm feels like a temporary release of the pain. However, it is a dangerous one that can lead to severe physical issues and more emotional harm.

Cutting, burning, or scratching oneself are the most frequent types of self-harm. The acts are usually done on the arms, legs, chest, and belly. However, any area of the body may be targeted, and by different methods. Often, youth hide the scabs or scars with their clothing and feel shame about what they have done, but they cannot stop themselves from doing it. The temporary relief that self-harm gives is outweighed by the long-term physical and emotional effects. Youth self-harm can result in wounds, scars, infections, nerve damage, severe burns, and broken bones. Young people who engage in self-harm often try to hide their actions from others, which in turn can increase feelings of loneliness, shame, and guilt, and thus add to the stress they are already experiencing.

Self-harm is more common among girls than boys, but all youth are at risk. According to a 2018 report in the *American Journal of Public Health*, rates of self-harm ranged from 6.4 to 14.8 percent for boys and 17.7 to 30.8 percent for girls. Self-harm by youth increased significantly during the first year of the

COVID-19 pandemic. FAIR Health, a national nonprofit organization that studies and reports on health care costs and health insurance claims, tracked claims from January to November 2020 compared to the same months in 2019. Claims to insurance for coverage of care for intentional self-harm as a percentage of all medical claims for thirteen- to eighteen-year-olds increased by almost 91 percent from March 2019 to March 2020.

At age sixteen, Alicia Moore was a straight-A student. Although known by her friends as both fun and smart, some of her classmates made fun of her for being such a good student. The teasing and harassment had been going on for years—and it made Moore feel sad and alone. In an effort to deal with her feelings, she began cutting in the fifth grade. "I ripped the soda can in half and I just cut myself," Moore explains. "I just remember kind of looking down and be like, 'I did that.' And I just remembered just having kind

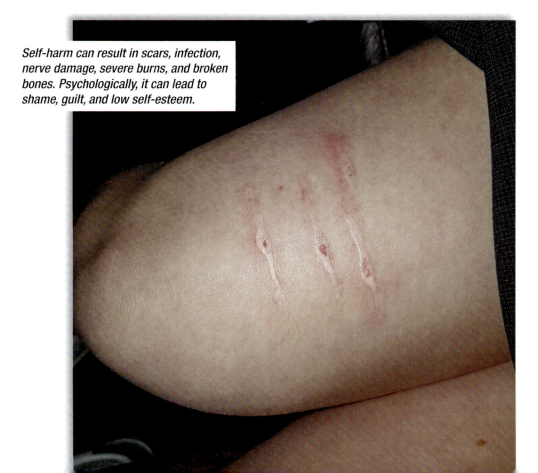

Self-harm can result in scars, infection, nerve damage, severe burns, and broken bones. Psychologically, it can lead to shame, guilt, and low self-esteem.

of this euphoric [feeling that], everything's okay."[11] From then on, whenever she felt low or stressed, she cut.

For years Moore turned to self-mutilation. She cut herself with razor blades, safety pins, and scissors. She hated herself for doing it, she confesses, but could not stop. "I didn't cut myself to try to kill myself. I cut myself to release all of this emotional pain that I felt like I couldn't handle anymore,"[12] she says. It would have continued, Moore says, except her mother found and read her diary. At that point her mother confronted her and helped her find a counselor. Moore worked hard in therapy to learn healthy ways to cope with negative emotions. Her doctor also started her on antidepressants. Today she no longer self-harms, and she has learned tools to deal with negative thoughts and stress.

> "I didn't cut myself to try to kill myself. I cut myself to release all of this emotional pain that I felt like I couldn't handle anymore."[12]
>
> —Alicia Moore, teen who self-harmed

Turning to Suicide

The worst possible outcome for youth struggling with mental health disorders is when their hopelessness and pain reach the point that they believe suicide is the only answer. Suicidal ideation occurs when individuals begin considering ending their life as the solution to their problems. It may include thoughts about how suicide could stop their pain, or it may include actual planning, in which the person decides how he or she will carry out the act.

Youth may consider suicide when they experience feelings of emptiness or hopelessness or when they see themselves as a burden to family or friends. At this point, some feel trapped and without any options—which is a dangerous place to be. Outward signs of these feelings may include retreating from family and friends, exhibiting severe mood swings, giving away valuables to friends, taking dangerous risks, or telling family and friends good-bye.

The number of teens and young adults who consider suicide and those who actually end their lives has been significantly increasing in the past two decades. According to the National Center for Health

Test Anxiety

When it comes to tests, many high school and college students experience stress. They might have trouble sleeping the night before a big test. They might feel jumpy or nervous on the morning of the test. But once the test begins, their emotions settle and they get to work. For other students tests bring about extreme and seemingly uncontrollable anxiety, a condition known as test anxiety. The symptoms of test anxiety include a racing heart, inability to concentrate, and rapid breathing. These symptoms make it difficult to do well on a test even when the student spent time studying and preparing for it. "When I experience it, it feels like my heart begins to race and I convince myself that I can't do anything and I'm going to fail the test," Karina Barron, a sophomore at Tarrant County College–Southeast Campus in Texas, says. "I do make jokes about it, but nobody knows the severity of what I think about before a test." Today many high schools and colleges offer services for those who deal with test anxiety, as well as counselors to help diagnose it.

Quoted in Katherine Osumah, "Students, Staff Weigh In on Test Anxiety," The Collegian, March 8, 2023. https://collegian.tccd.edu.

Statistics, from 2009 to 2019 the proportion of high school students who contemplated suicide increased by 36 percent. Those who created a suicide plan increased by 44 percent. The rise in suicides and suicidal thoughts has continued for teens and young adults. CDC reports from 2020 and 2021 reveal an 8 percent increase in suicides among males aged fifteen to twenty-four and a 5 percent increase for females in the same age group. These increases led to hundreds more deaths by suicide per year for these age groups.

Surviving the Unimaginable

The feeling of hopelessness that leads someone to consider or carry out suicide is unimaginable to many people. In 2022 Waylon Griswold shared his story of surviving a suicide attempt the previous year. Griswold had experienced depression since his teens and had been hospitalized in a youth psychiatric hospital at age seventeen because of his self-harming. The self-harm occurred after years of dealing with chronic post-traumatic stress disorder and depression. He had grown up with his grandmother, who adopted him. When she realized he was hurting himself, she called the police, which led to Griswold being hospitalized.

While he felt okay for a while afterward, his chronic depression started to return. In 2021, at age twenty-three, he felt like he had no future. He told his grandmother he was going for a walk to the nearby lighthouse, which is 15 to 20 feet (4.6 to 6.1 m) high. Griswold writes:

> I walked to the lighthouse and climbed up the steps. I called 911 and they tried to talk me out of it, but I was tired of my life. I felt as if I was a burden or not good enough for my family. I was in and out of psychiatric hospitals, I felt hopeless, and I believed, in that moment, that suicide would take my problems away. I put the phone down on the ground and sat on the edge of the railing. I was scared and shaking but I jumped.[13]

Youth considering suicide are at the point of feeling hopeless, trapped, and without any other options.

Griswold landed on his feet on the concrete. At first the adrenaline coursed through him, and he felt no pain. But it soon became apparent that his jump had caused serious injuries. "I broke my back, shattered my feet, had to have numerous surgeries with screws, rods and plates inserted into my body. I was in a wheelchair for several months. Infections followed and more hospital stays were needed. But I survived,"[14] Griswold writes. He realized that because he had called 911, there was some hope in him that he would survive and get help. And he did receive help. He underwent a year of intense treatment, both for his physical and emotional state. At the conclusion of this treatment, he writes, he no longer saw suicide as an option.

Whereas Griswold recovered from the suicide attempt, he continues to have to work to maintain his mental health. It is an ongoing struggle. Depression and hopelessness can resurface, which means that those who experience these feelings need to be vigilant. They need to learn how to recognize their feelings, the signs of distress, and when to seek professional help.

CHAPTER TWO

Causes of the Crisis

Anxiety, depression, and suicide have been rising for over a decade among youth, with health care professionals calling for action to address the crisis. Many studies and experts contend that the COVID-19 pandemic exacerbated youth's mental health issues, although the problem was already serious before that. Even after the pandemic lockdowns were lifted, youth continued to exhibit troubling mental health issues. The roots of these issues are often complex and can be tied to lack of connections, poor self-worth, bullying, genetics, trauma, and other factors.

Lack of Connections

Lack of connections or interactions with others is one factor that can affect a youth's mental health and is linked to anxiety and depression. The COVID-19 lockdowns or being a new student at a school or even starting college are just some examples of situations that can lead to youth feeling disconnected from others and without a support group. Any situation in which a person lacks dependable bonds with others or reoccurring connections can affect mental health. A 2022 report published in the *Community Mental Health Journal* found that among university faculty, staff, and students, levels of anxiety and depression were much greater in those who were socially isolated. The lack of bonds can lead to, or worsen, mental health issues such as anxiety or depression.

Victoria Canales experienced this as a nineteen-year-old college student during the pandemic. One night while alone in her apartment near campus, she contemplated taking her own life. Although in-person college classes had resumed, in-person social events were not yet allowed. Most students just stayed in their apartments and dorm rooms. Canales was supposed to have a roommate, but the roommate chose to stay at home. This left Canales alone much of the time. Canales's grades were slipping, and she felt like she had no one to talk to. That night she decided to call the campus crisis hotline and spoke with a woman who was manning the hotline. "I told them 'I'm feeling pretty bad. I'm not doing too well in my classes and I'd kind of just like someone to talk to,'"[15] she explains. She talked with the crisis line staffer for over an hour; a mental health counselor was then sent to check on her. With additional professional help, Canales decided to make changes in her life. She started taking medication for depression and spent more time with people who shared her interest in music.

The long months with little or no social interaction caused some young people to develop so much anxiety that they kind of forgot how to connect with others. When universities reopened, Nevandria Page, age twenty-five, moved to Ottawa, Canada, to pursue a master's degree in feminist and gender studies. At the beginning she was excited to explore a new city. But whenever she went out, she felt nervous and as though everyone was staring at her. It got to the point that she feared having to leave her house. Going into a café and trying to order a coffee caused her to stutter. "I was alone throughout the pandemic, and I think that feeling of loneliness followed me, despite being able to go out again,"[16] Page says. Her previous isolation and feelings of loneliness increased the anxiety she still feels, even with the ability to interact. Without continuing connections and interactions, a person is more at risk of developing mental health issues, such as happened with Page.

> "I was alone throughout the pandemic, and I think that feeling of loneliness followed me, despite being able to go out again."[16]
>
> —Nevandria Page, graduate student

The COVID-19 lockdowns led to youth feeling disconnected with others and without a support group. Any situation where a person lacks dependable bonds with others can affect mental health.

Bullying

Just as a lack of connections can aggravate mental health, so can negative interactions like bullying. Bullying, whether it occurs online or in person, can have a major impact on the mental health of young people. Bullies typically rely on insults and demeaning actions to humiliate and harm their victims.

In-person bullying can include verbal attacks such as name-calling, physical attacks such as hitting, threatening the person, or excluding the person from activities. Bullying in person most often occurs at school by classmates. Many students have experienced this. According to the 2023 CDC Youth Risk Behavior Survey, approximately 15 percent of students surveyed in 2021 reported that they were bullied at school. Increasingly, bullying is occurring online, particularly on social media. Almost half of US teens aged thirteen to seventeen reported that they had experienced at least one of six cyberbullying behaviors that were

The Bully

Bullying adversely affects the one who is bullied, but studies have shown that bullies also often experience poor mental health. A 2019 Swedish study by professors at Örebro University found that young people involved in cyberbullying—whether the victim or the bully—were at increased risk for depression and anxiety. Other studies have had similar findings. "Bullies themselves suffer consequences from their actions," writes Nadra Nittle, a journalist who covers issues including mental health. "They, too, have an increased risk of substance use disorders and quitting school. In addition, they tend to have more physical fights, engage in sexual activity at younger ages, and enter the criminal justice system."

Nadra Nittle, "Why Do People Bully?," Verywell Mind, July 31, 2021. www.verywellmind.com.

included in a 2022 Pew Research Center survey. The six behaviors bullies use included offensive name-calling; spreading false rumors about the victim; sending explicit images to the victim that they didn't ask for; physical threats; constantly being asked where they are, what they're doing, or who they're with; and having explicit images of them shared without their consent.

Being bullied is linked to an increased likelihood of mental health disorders—in particular, anxiety issues. Psychologists contend that bullying can lead to feelings of shame, low self-esteem, adjustment problems, and even getting sick from the stress. A 2022 research paper published in the *Journal of Affective Disorders* reported that of the 2,155 adolescents surveyed, 16.5 percent said that they had experienced different levels of bullying in the past months. The study also found that adolescents who had been bullied had higher severity scores for depression and anxiety.

Parents have seen the effects on their kids. "My sixteen year old son was cyber bullied on Facebook over a period of 8 hours," one parent shared in an email with the Cyberbullying Research Center. "The event was so traumatic it caused my son to have an acute psychotic break and to be hospitalized in an adolescent psychiatric ward for almost a month. He is changed forever and will never be the same mentally. Internet bullying can hurt and affect people and kids need to know this."[17]

In the worst cases, bullying can be a contributing factor in youth committing suicide. Terry Badger III, of Indiana, had dreamed of playing major league baseball for his favorite team, the St. Louis Cardinals. His parents say he was both kind and outgoing. But in 2023, at just thirteen years old, Terry took his own life. His parents say he was repeatedly bullied at his middle school. In the last moments of life, he recorded a video on his cell phone, naming the bullies at school and blaming them for his decision to commit suicide. "He was being made fun of all the time," his mother, Robyn Badger, says. "[They] put him down, told him he was a loser. Told him he was fat and that he should kill himself. Kids told him he sucked at baseball. Every haircut he had they made fun of."[18] Terry's parents had met with school staff twice that school year to ask for help to stop the bullying, but the bullying continued. Terry's suicide left his family heartbroken.

> "[They] put him down, told him he was a loser. Told him he was fat and that he should kill himself."[18]
>
> —Robyn Badger, mother of Terry Badger III, who took his own life at age thirteen

Psychologists contend that bullying can lead to feelings of shame, low self-esteem, adjustment problems, and even getting sick from stress.

Social Media Impacts

Social media has also been blamed for contributing to the mental health crisis among teens. Most teens have access to the latest digital devices—and they spend a lot of time on those devices. A 2022 Pew Research Center survey of 1,316 teens found that most had access to digital devices, with 95 percent having access to a smartphone, 90 percent to a desktop or laptop computer, and 80 percent to a gaming console. Not surprisingly, the same survey found that teens spend large amounts of time online. Ninety-seven percent of teens say they use the internet daily, with 52 percent of fifteen- to seventeen-year-olds reporting that they use the internet almost constantly, and 36 percent of thirteen- to fourteen-year-olds saying the same. Much of their online time is spent on social media. The most popular sites among teens, according to the survey, are YouTube, TikTok, Instagram, and Snapchat.

On social media, many teens compare their own lives to the lives of their peers. Or they get caught up in comparing how many social media likes they get versus how many likes their friends and acquaintances get.

While social media can be a positive force in a teen's life—enabling them to form positive online relationships with like-minded peers—it can also pose risks. Many teens compare their own lives (which to them seem positively boring) to the lives of other teens posting on social media (which seem absolutely exciting and glamorous). Or they get caught up in comparing how many likes they get versus how many likes their friends and acquaintances get. Another risk factor is that they isolate themselves, spending much of their time with online activities rather than engaging in school and other activities and forming in-person friendships. All of this can lead to stress and low self-esteem, fueling problems such as anxiety.

Those who are on social media excessively are most at risk for these types of stresses. A 2019 study by the Johns Hopkins Bloomberg School of Public Health detailed the risks. That study of more than sixty-five hundred American young people aged twelve to fifteen found that those who spent more than three hours a day using social media had heightened risk for mental health problems. Another 2019 study, this one involving more than twelve thousand English thirteen- to sixteen-year-olds, found that use of social media over three times a day was a predictor of poor mental health and well-being in teens.

Emma Lembke and Aliza Kopans are familiar with the emotional minefield that can be social media. It was their experiences with social media as middle school students that led the two college sophomores to lobby in 2022 for new regulations and safeguards. Lembke was using social media in the eighth grade and recalls that year as her worst in terms of mental health. She was constantly comparing herself to others online and checking her "likes" to see if people were responding to her posts. Kopans also experienced negative effects when she started following social media at age twelve. "I went on YouTube and fell into these harmful rabbit holes that caused me to actually have disordered eating," Kopans explains. She says that the social media companies "didn't care that I would count my likes and followers and quantify my worth consistently for years and that led to increased rates of anxiety and depression. They didn't care as long as my eyes were on the screen and as long as I was making them profit."[19] Lembke and Kopans are continuing to work toward regulations that will help prevent these types of outcomes in other young people.

Dealing with Difficulties

Life outside of social media can also be full of stressors for teens. What is going on in a young person's life significantly affects his or her mental health positively or negatively, depending on the circumstances. Stress is a normal part of a person's life. Taking a test, waiting to hear about a college application, or arguing with a best friend can all lead to anxiety and stress. But these types of stress are often resolved at some point. Chronic stress, which is experiencing stress constantly with no resolution for a long period, negatively impacts the mental health of youth. Chronic stress could result from constant worrying about grades, dealing with parents undergoing a divorce, or overextending oneself with sports, clubs, a job, and academics. The problem is that chronic stress can lead to or worsen anxiety, depression, sleep problems, and substance abuse. For students, academic pressures can be a major factor in chronic stress. A 2022 study of 843 college students published in *Frontiers in Psychology* examined the connection between perceived levels of academic stress and mental well-being. The study found that there was an association between serious academic stress and poor mental well-being.

Trauma also can severely affect a young person's mental health. Trauma results from extremely stressful events that destroy a young person's sense of security and often result in feelings of loneliness and fear. Living in foster care; physical, sexual, or verbal abuse; and the death of a parent or other loved one are examples of traumatic events that some teens experience. According to the US Department of Health and Human Services, more than two-thirds of young people experience at least one traumatic event by age sixteen.

Homelessness and Mental Health

Young people who are homeless or are at risk for becoming homeless lack physical and emotional security. One in ten young adults ages eighteen to twenty-five and one in thirty adolescents ages thirteen to seventeen experience some form of homelessness, according to a 2023 report by Chapin Hall at the University of Chicago. These teens and young adults are more likely to experience mental health issues than their peers who have stable homes. The National Clearinghouse on Homeless Youth and Families reports that 45 percent of homeless students experience depression. In contrast, 27 percent of students who live in stable homes experience depression.

As a result, homeless youth or those at risk for homelessness have increased rates of mental health issues, which include depression and anxiety, compared to youth living in stable homes. "If you are a homeless youth, you are going to be stressed, be depressed," says Heather Beaule, a care coordinator at Waypoint, a program that works with homeless youth. "Sometimes they have parents who are incarcerated or have substance use problems. In one of my cases, the person lost her mother. The dad wanted nothing to do with her. She grew up on the streets. Some of these kids are on the streets as young as 14 years old."

Quoted in Karen Dandurant, "Waypoint SleepOut 2023: Care Coordinators Speak Up on Need to Help Homeless Youth," Fosters, March 13, 2023. www.fosters.com.

For Liz Sanders, a blogger and artist, growing up with chaos and abuse resulted in her trauma. Her family life was often chaotic, punctuated by loud arguments, verbal abuse, paranoia, and emotional outbursts by family members. Sanders writes:

By middle school, I was deeply depressed (as was everyone in my family). I would soldier on through the day, pretending everything was fine. Practically every night, I would cry myself to sleep. Once the door was shut and the lights were off, only then would I allow myself to feel all the anger, sorrow and loneliness growing inside me, bubbling just beneath the surface. I experimented with self-harm as a way to validate the invisible and intangible suffering.[20]

It was not until she got to college that Sanders was able to get a handle on the anxiety and depression she felt while living at home. Getting away from the actual trauma was the first step, but her healing took much more time and therapy to process the years of discord.

The Role of Biology

Genetics can also play a role in mental health. Certain mental illnesses, such as bipolar disorder, have been linked to genetics. In a study done by researchers at Yale University and the US Department of Veterans Affairs and published in 2021, scientists reviewed the health records of more than 1.2 million people to look for genetic patterns of depression. This study identified 178 gene locations in DNA that are connected to major depression.

> "We've known for many years that risk for depression is genetically influenced. There's an environmental component to risk, which includes things like adverse life events, and there's a genetic component to the risk."[21]
>
> —Joel Gelernter, Foundations Fund Professor of Psychiatry at Yale University

Scientists believe this knowledge will one day help determine who is more at risk for depression, which could lead to earlier treatment. "We've known for many years that risk for depression is genetically influenced," says study coauthor Joel Gelernter, Foundations Fund Professor of Psychiatry at Yale University. "There's an environmental component to risk, which includes things like adverse life events, and there's a genetic component to the risk. It's only relatively recently that we, in the field, have started to identify what some of the specific risk genes and risk variants are."[21]

Understanding the various causes of mental health problems can help lead to earlier interventions and better treatments. This, in turn, can enhance strategies for coping and recovery.

CHAPTER THREE

Most Vulnerable Youth

While any and all teens are susceptible to the mental health crisis, recent studies have shown that LGBTQ youth, female teens, and young people of color are particularly at risk for mental health disorders. Young people in these groups are more vulnerable to depression, anxiety, and other emotional issues because they are more likely than others to experience assault, racism or bias, and physical harm (or threat of it). Along with the factors that increase their risk of mental health problems, youth in these groups are less likely to have protective factors, such as close relationships with peers, in their lives. As an example, the 2023 CDC Youth Risk Behavior Survey reported that young people in these groups were less likely to feel connected at school, which feeling is a major protective factor against mental health problems. This lack of protection for LGBTQ, female, and Black youth and the stresses they endure mean the mental health crisis is particularly relevant for them.

LGBTQ Teens at Risk

LGBTQ teens are more likely to have negative thoughts about themselves than other young people. The 2023 Youth Risk Behavior Survey reported that 69 percent of LGBTQ teens surveyed said they had persistent feelings of sadness, and 45 percent said they had considered attempting suicide. These feelings are even more difficult to deal with without support from home, a key problem for LGBTQ youth.

Family support is a key protective factor in reducing the risk of mental health problems. The Trevor Project, a nonprofit national organization dedicated to protecting LGBTQ youth, surveyed more than thirty-five thousand LGBTQ youth for a study published in 2022. It found that youth who reported high levels of support from their families attempted suicide at less than half the rate of those who felt low or moderate levels of support. The problem is that many families are not supportive of their LGBTQ members. As an example, the Trevor Project also reported that fewer than one in three transgender and nonbinary youth found their home to be gender-affirming.

Another stressor in the lives of LGBTQ teens is having to deal with bullying and threats of physical harm. The 2023 CDC Youth Risk Behavior Survey reported that more than one in ten LGBTQ students had skipped school because they feared for their personal safety. Almost one in four experienced sexual violence, and nearly one in four were bullied at school. The 2022 Trevor Project survey had similar findings. According to that survey, 36 percent of LGBTQ youth experienced physical threats or harm due to their sexual orientation or gender identity.

Bullied for Being Himself

Eli Fritchley was twelve years old and in seventh grade at Cascades Middle School in Tennessee in 2021 when, according to his parents, he was badly bullied for just being himself. Eli played trombone in marching band, painted his nails, liked the color pink, and let other students know that he was gay. "He was told because he didn't necessarily have a religion, and that he said he was gay, that he was going to go to Hell. They told him that quite often,"[22] says his mother, Debbey Fritchley. She said he sometimes cried because of the mean comments made by other kids, but she and her husband did not realize the trauma he suffered from the taunts.

Persistent Feelings of Sadness or Hopelessness in Teens

While many US teens are experiencing persistent feelings of sadness or hopelessness, certain groups of teens are suffering more than others. This is the finding of a survey conducted by the Centers for Disease Control and Prevention and published in February 2023. The survey is done every two years among a nationally representative sampling of students in public and private high schools. According to the survey, the most troubled groups include teen girls, LGBTQ teens, and multiracial and Hispanic teens.

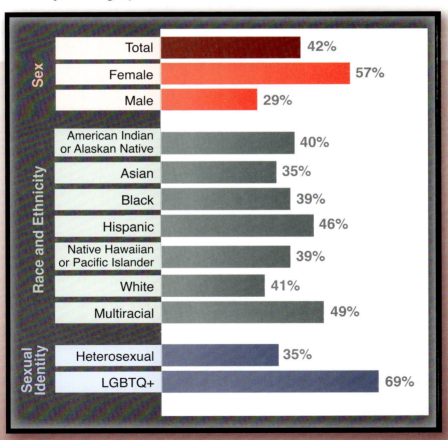

Percentage of High School Students Who Experienced Persistent Feelings of Sadness or Hopelessness During the Past Year, by Demographic Characteristics, United States, 2021

Sex
- Total: 42%
- Female: 57%
- Male: 29%

Race and Ethnicity
- American Indian or Alaskan Native: 40%
- Asian: 35%
- Black: 39%
- Hispanic: 46%
- Native Hawaiian or Pacific Islander: 39%
- White: 41%
- Multiracial: 49%

Sexual Identity
- Heterosexual: 35%
- LGBTQ+: 69%

Source: "Youth Risk Behavior Survey: Data Summary & Trends Report: 2011–2021," Centers for Disease Control and Prevention's Division of Adolescent and School Health, February 13, 2023. www.cdc.gov.

On November 28, 2021, Debbey walked into her son's bedroom and found that Eli had committed suicide. It was only then that Eli's parents realized how much their son had been suffering. "It was really abusive," his father, Steve Fritchley, says. "I don't think it was ever physical. I think it was just words, but words hurt."[23] Eli's sense of self was destroyed by the ugly and deeply painful comments from his peers.

Some LGBTQ youth are able to overcome the abuses directed at them. Alex Singh was in fifth grade when he understood who he was. While assigned female at birth, inside he felt like a boy. He talked about how puberty is the hardest time for a transgender person because their body is becoming what they do not want to be. By age thirteen, with his parents' help, he formally began to transition. He legally changed his name and started dressing and presenting as a male. He did this surrounded by classmates who had always known him as a female, and among those classmates, he has a small group of close friends. While not subject to overt bullying, there are classmates who refer to him as "it" and are not supportive. Singh deals with this with different strategies, such as by using his imagination. "I definitely get depressed sometimes," he says. "I have my imaginary world and that's one of my coping strategies. Like when I'm feeling down and depressed, I go into my imaginary world, and in my imaginary world, I am a guy, I have a flat chest, I'm strong."[24]

While his parents are supportive, they are nervous about starting puberty blockers that would help pause his puberty from progressing. For Singh, his developing female body gives him negative feelings about himself. Dealing with others' reactions and dealing with a body that does not match how he feels make it difficult for Singh to always feel positive about

"I definitely get depressed sometimes. I have my imaginary world and that's one of my coping strategies. Like when I'm feeling down and depressed, I go into my imaginary world, and in my imaginary world, I am a guy."[24]

—Alex Singh, teenage transgender male

Effects of So-Called Conversion Therapy

A serious danger to the mental health of LGBTQ young people is being subjected to a procedure called conversion therapy. Conversion therapy is a discredited practice intended to convert LGBTQ individuals to being heterosexual or cisgender. These practices are discredited by professional organizations such as the American Medical Association and are considered a detriment to mental health. A 2022 report supported by the Trevor Project analyzed twenty-eight published studies and found that 12 percent of the LGBTQ individuals surveyed had experienced conversion therapy. Compared to LGBTQ individuals in the study who did not undergo the conversion practices, recipients experienced serious psychological distress (47 percent versus 34 percent), depression (65 percent versus 27 percent), substance abuse (67 percent versus 50 percent), and attempted suicide (58 percent versus 39 percent).

Sean Cahill is director of health policy research at the Fenway Institute, a health association that advocates for LGBTQ people's health in Boston. He says, "I think it's really important for parents to know that if they have their child do conversion therapy, their child has greater odds of experiencing serious psychological distress, depression, substance use and suicide. I would think that a lot of parents would not be happy to learn that."

Quoted in Jen Christiansen, "Conversion Therapy Is Harmful to LGBTQ People and Costs Society as a Whole, Study Says," CNN, March 7, 2022. www.cnn.com.

himself. However, because he does have affirming parents and friends, has coping strategies, and sees a therapist, he has been able to maintain his mental health with their help.

Teen Girls

Another group of young Americans that is experiencing rising difficulties with mental health is teenage girls. In February 2023 the CDC published a survey in which 57 percent of high school girls reported persistent feelings of sadness or hopelessness, an increase from 36 percent in 2011 and nearly twice the rate reported by males in the same age group.

One main reason for young women's increased reports of mental health issues is sexual assault. According to the same survey, 18 percent of female teens said they experienced sexual violence. This contrasts with 11 percent of all teens (male and female) who reported being the victims of sexual violence. Additionally, more than one in ten girls reported that they had been forced to have sex. "That is just an overwhelming finding," says Kathleen Ethier, director of the CDC's Division of Adolescent and School Health. "So, not surprisingly, we're also seeing that almost 60 percent of teen girls had depressive symptoms in the past year, which is the highest level in a decade."[25]

For Ky, a student at Colorado State University in 2022, being violated in high school led to panic attacks and low self-esteem for years after the assault. When she was a high school junior, Ky took a weekend trip with a few male and female friends. During the trip, the teens—Ky included—drank a lot of alcohol. This was her first experience getting drunk. While she was in that state, some of the guys pressured her to go into a bedroom, and two of them sexually assaulted her. They finally stopped when she threw up.

Ky stayed at the cabin the rest of the weekend, never mentioning what had happened to anyone. More than a year later, while at college, she finally talked about what had happened to her. She took a class on sexual assault that all students at Colorado State University take during their freshman orientation. After the class, she experienced a panic attack and started crying. Ky writes:

> I truly didn't realize that I was assaulted, the whole time I thought that I did something wrong and bad and that I deserved it. And that is just what guys did to pretty girls, and that they were my friends so it couldn't be assault. I've always hated myself for putting myself through this, and it's so much harder to blame the people that caused your pain when you believe it's your fault. I had never had sex or any kind of intimacy before that other than kissing. Sex has been something that I have steered away from out of fear ever since that night.[26]

Teenage girls are experiencing rising difficulties with mental health. A 2023 survey revealed 57 percent of high school girls reported persistent feelings of hopelessness, an increase from 36 percent in 2011.

Even after finally realizing that the assault was not her fault and being able to open up about what happened, Ky is still experiencing the emotional effects of that night. She continues to experience shame and finds it difficult to trust people. She says she is taking steps to combat the pain it caused, sharing her experience and talking about it, but the pain is still with her every day. Teenage girls are subjected to other pressures that threaten their mental health. Social media is the source of many of these pressures. All teens, but especially girls, are bombarded by images of the perfect face, the perfect body, and the perfect life. They compare their looks, grades, weight, "likes," social activities, clothes, and just about everything about themselves with others online. Doing this can damage self-esteem, lead to depression, anxiety, and eating disorders. Internal research done by Facebook in 2020 revealed that 32 percent of teen girls said that scrolling through Instagram (which is owned by Facebook) when they felt bad about their bodies made them feel even worse. "You're scrolling through it at your house and seeing what others are doing and it can make you feel left out, or others feel left out,"[27] explains teenager Violet Boehler.

People of Color

The third group of young Americans who have been identified as experiencing mental health problems are teens of color. In particular, Black teenagers are experiencing alarming rates of suicide and depression. The 2023 CDC Youth Risk Behavior Survey revealed that 39 percent of Black youth surveyed felt persistent feelings of hopelessness and sadness, compared to 27 percent in 2011. Additionally, from 2013 to 2019, the suicide rate of Black young men ages fifteen to twenty-four increased by 47 percent, and by 59 percent for Black young women of the same age.

Mental health professionals attribute the rise in mental health issues among Black teens and young adults to racism, violence, food insecurity, interactions with police, and lack of access to mental health care. "You have to bring culture into this, you have to talk about racism, you have to talk about discrimination," says Arielle Sheftall, a principal investigator at the Center for Suicide Prevention and Research at Nationwide Children's Hospital in Columbus, Ohio. "It is something that Black youth experience every single day."[28] As an example, in Cleveland, Ohio, the school district is about two-thirds Black. CDC data from 2019 showed that approximately 18 percent of Cleveland high school students had attempted suicide in the past twelve months, compared with 9 percent of students nationwide. Many Cleveland students experience chronic stressors, including neighborhood violence and food insecurity, which contribute to mental health issues.

During the first years of the COVID-19 pandemic, Joy Menh, a student at Hum-

> "You have to bring culture into this, you have to talk about racism, you have to talk about discrimination. It is something that Black youth experience every single day."[28]
>
> —Arielle Sheftall, a principal investigator at the Center for Suicide Prevention and Research at Nationwide Children's Hospital in Columbus, Ohio

Mental health professionals attribute some of the rise in mental health issues among Black teens to interactions with police, violence, and racism.

boldt State University and the daughter of immigrants from Liberia, dealt with the isolation of remote learning, worry about her parents contracting COVID-19, financial stress, and the challenge of balancing work and studies. Then her mental health took a major hit when the murder of George Floyd, a Black man, occurred at the hands of police. Many people watched the video of this incident, prompting protests against racism around the country. "I can discuss it, but it's very hard for me to see these Black deaths continue happening," she says. "There's so much craziness, it's hard for me to focus."[29] Menh turned to her college's counseling office and found this helpful for her state of mind. She has found another way to cope with her stress: she works at the campus multicultural center, where she helps other Black students.

Lack of Treatment

Not getting treatment is also a factor in the rising mental health crisis, which is a major problem for people of color. A 2020 study

An issue with Black youth seeking mental health counseling is that the percentage of Black psychological professionals is relatively small. Some Black youth would prefer a Black counselor because they want a person who understands the racism they have dealt with, or because their community discourages seeing someone who is not Black. The American Psychological Association found that just 4 percent of US psychologists are Black, even though Black people make up 13 percent of the population. A similar difference exists with social workers and counselors. "This is a deterrent," says Dr. Kali D. Cyrus, a Black psychiatrist at Sibley Memorial Hospital in Washington, DC. "Talking about your family's business with a white person—much less an outsider—is often discouraged in the Black community." Without this situation changing, it is another obstacle to improving mental health in Black teens.

Quoted in Joel Abrams, "African American Teens Face Mental Health Crisis but Are Less Likely than Whites to Get Treatment," The Conversation, July 29, 2020. https://thecon versation.com.

by the School of Nursing at the University of Texas at Austin found that about 9 percent of Black youth in the study reported a major depression episode in the past year, but only about 40 percent of these youth obtained treatment. Comparatively, about 46 percent of White youth who reported a depressive episode were treated. According to the American Psychiatric Association, some studies indicate one reason for the lack of treatment is that Black youth with psychiatric disorders are more likely to be referred to the juvenile justice system, whereas White youth are more likely to be referred for mental health treatment.

Another reason for the disparity in treatment is that there has been a stigma in the Black community regarding getting mental health help. Myah White, a high school student in California, explains that she and her friends of color find seeking help can sometimes feel hard because of how mental illness is seen in their community. "Depression and anxiety are things you don't always talk about in the Black community," says White. "Our parents are dealing with their own trauma. You just want to be 'normal.' With so many hardships, we want to be known for perseverance and strength."[30] To process her stress about racism and other issues, White got involved in working on diversity issues at her school. Doing so allowed her to share her emotions with others with similar experiences. Her involvement also allowed her to educate her non-Black classmates about racism. The ability to talk, share, and educate others helped White cope with the stressors in her life.

For White and others in these vulnerable groups, it is imperative that they have access to mental health care, from getting help developing coping strategies to getting medical treatment. As the youth mental health crisis continues, particular attention must be paid to LGBTQ young people, teenage girls, and young people of color in order that their mental health, as a whole, improves.

CHAPTER FOUR

What Can Be Done to Ease the Teen Mental Health Crisis?

With millions of American young people experiencing depression, anxiety, and other debilitating conditions, health professionals warn that the mental health crisis is at a critical point. The 2021 US surgeon general's report *Protecting Youth Mental Health* noted that 25 percent of youth experienced depressive symptoms and 20 percent experienced anxiety symptoms. The report sounded another alarm when it noted that in early 2021 US emergency department visits for suspected suicide attempts were 51 percent higher for adolescent girls and 4 percent higher for adolescent boys compared with 2019. Despite these daunting statistics, mental health professionals believe there is a way forward that can help millions of youth.

Experts have studied preventive and intervention protocols that have shown success. To make an impact, however, they need to be implemented nationwide. "To be sure, this isn't an issue we can fix overnight or with a single prescription," writes US surgeon general Vivek H. Murthy. "Ensuring healthy children and families will take an all-of-society effort, including policy, institutional, and individual changes in how we view and prioritize mental health."[31]

The surgeon general's office, CDC, and other professional health organizations believe there are key programs and actions that will mitigate mental health issues. These include ensuring there is widespread access to mental health counseling, increasing proactive mental health programs in schools, reducing risk factors, and involving youth in helping one another.

Access to Counseling

One of the ways to provide help to youth is to ensure they are able to readily access counseling for any mental health need. The primary way to do this is through the schools, where youth spend much of their time. Additionally, school-based services reduce barriers such as transportation and health insurance that may keep teens from getting needed services.

Currently, one issue is the lack of school counselors, which makes it more difficult to support children dealing with mental health challenges. The American School Counselor Association recommends one counselor for every 250 students, but as of 2021 the national average was one counselor for every 408 students. The US surgeon general recommends more funding at the federal and state level for mental health counseling in public schools. The American Rescue Plan, which was signed into law in 2021, led to a 65 percent increase in school social workers and a 17 percent increase in counselors, relative to before the pandemic. The added number of social workers and counselors in schools is helping but, experts say, even more are needed.

For Emma F., reaching out to her school counselor helped her gain control of anxious feelings that developed during pandemic lockdowns—an event that coincided with her parents going through a divorce. During her freshman year in high school, while attending virtual school, she reached out to her counselor via email,

"Ensuring healthy children and families will take an all-of-society effort, including policy, institutional, and individual changes in how we view and prioritize mental health."[31]

—Vivek H. Murthy, US surgeon general

A shortage of school counselors makes it more difficult to support children dealing with mental health challenges. In 2021, the national average was one counselor for every 408 students.

nervous about whether it was the right action. Emma soon found that talking to her counselor helped her cope with the negative emotions that arose from the stresses in her life. She continued to speak with the counselor on a regular basis throughout her sophomore year. During that year, when her father decided to remarry, seeing the counselor helped her deal with the difficult emotions resulting from his remarriage.

Emma's counselor changed in the 2022–2023 school year, and as a junior she had to get used to a new counselor. But she confided in the new counselor, and it helped save her life. "It was a Friday, after school, and I had a terrible day with three panic attacks," writes Emma. "I was supposed to have speech practice after school but instead wanted to run and drown myself at the lake. That day, there must have been a little part of me that wanted to live because I went and talked to my counselor. She called my mom, and my mom came to talk with us to ensure my safety."[32] Emma writes more about how seeing a counselor is a sign of strength and that it means you are taking control of your life. She says that counseling has helped her find her way through major difficulties.

Emergency Hotlines

In addition to counseling availability, teens need to know about emergency services if they reach a crisis situation. All teens need to be aware of hotlines for mental health crisis help in order to reduce the chances of self-harm, suicide, and other harmful actions. There are national, local, and school hotlines. There are hotlines specific to LGBTQ crises, youth issues, and more. An example of a national hotline is the 988 Suicide & Crisis Lifeline (formerly known as the National Suicide Prevention Lifeline), which is available all day, every day by phone or text for anyone with suicidal thoughts or who feel in crisis. It also offers help for Spanish speakers and for people who are deaf or hard of hearing. Lifeline staff are trained to listen carefully, offer help with coping strategies, and connect callers with other resources as needed.

TikTok Help

While mental health professionals warn of the dangers of social media, there are positive aspects that can help youths' mental health journey. For one, social media can help them discover people dealing with issues like their own. Peter Wallerich-Neils, who is known as Peter Hyphen to his over 416,000 followers on TikTok, used TikTok to explain his diagnosis and journey with ADHD. "It's kind of holding a mirror up to themselves and they can realize, 'Oh, my gosh, I didn't realize that this is something that I thought only I dealt with'—knowing that there could be a name for it. And 'I am part of this community that I didn't even know existed,'" Wallerich-Neils explains. TikTok also provides mental health information from people like Kojo Sarfo, a mental health nurse practitioner and psychotherapist with over 3 million followers on TikTok. Sarfo says the app allows people with mental health conditions to feel like they belong. However, professionals like Sarfo warn that while TikTok is a good place to get information and connect, one should see a professional for an actual diagnosis of and treatment for any problem.

Quoted in Madalyn Amato, "TikTok Is Helping Gen Z with Mental Health. Here's What It Can and Can't Do," *Los Angeles Times*, January 5, 2022. www.latimes.com.

Studies show that crisis lines like these are effective in helping youth. A 2018 study in the *Journal of Affective Disorders* reported that young people who used a suicide prevention hotline experienced a significant decrease in suicidal thoughts and improved mood after calling and talking to someone. The major problem to overcome is making these hotlines known to youth. According to a 2019 national survey by the Substance Abuse and Mental Health Services Administration (SAMHSA), only 35.9 percent of youth aged twelve to seventeen reported that they were aware of a suicide-prevention hotline.

National and local governments have been increasing funding to help with awareness and accessibility of these hotlines. One example of this effort was to create a simpler number to remember and call for people trying to reach the National Suicide Prevention Lifeline. In 2022 SAMHSA announced $282 million in funding to transition the National Suicide Prevention Lifeline's ten-digit number to a three-digit dialing code, 988 — which occurred in July of that year. In August 2022 the 988 line answered 152,000 more contacts via calls, chats, and texts than it had in August 2021. Continued awareness campaigns of these hotlines are planned by federal, local, and educational organizations.

Proactive Mental Health Programs

While awareness of how to get help in a crisis situation is needed, mental health professionals also believe that young people need to be made aware of the mental health protective factors, how to recognize symptoms of someone in distress, and how to get help before a crisis occurs. One way to do so is by establishing mental health programs in the schools, since these enable students to recognize and seek help for themselves. These programs have become more common since 2021, when Congress passed a law that provided increased funding for states to use toward public school mental health programs.

In some schools, counselors create programs of their own. The programs aim to reduce the stigma of mental illness, and provide students information on how to get help, if needed.

Part of the funding has been to establish programs that proactively educate students on mental health. An increasing number of states have adopted legislation to include mental health as part of their public schools' K–12 health curricula. The goal is to help students understand their feelings, give them a way to talk about them, and seek help if needed. One of the states that added this to the curriculum is Rhode Island. In 2021, the state legislature passed a law that requires all school staff and students to receive education on suicide awareness and prevention. Another state, New Jersey, implemented legislation in 2020 that requires mental health education for kindergarten through twelfth grade in all state public schools. Other states have enacted or are considering similar types of laws to ensure more students receive mental health education.

Strong Relationships

A major way to ease the youth mental health crisis is for teens to develop close relationships with others. Strong relationships help reduce the onset of mental health problems and help people recognize early symptoms in order to start treatment. Studies have found that strong links between parents and peers offer protection from suicidal thoughts. This was the finding of a 2020 study published in *JAMA Network Open*. Study participants included 1,174 individuals aged nineteen and twenty. The study found that those who felt they had social support experienced fewer depressive and anxiety symptoms and suicide-related outcomes. For parents or guardians, this means reaching out and making efforts to talk to and listen to their teens. For teens themselves, trying to connect with peers of the same interests and pushing themselves to get off screens to develop in-person relationships would help their emotional well-being.

In some schools, counselors are creating programs of their own as they see the effects of the mental health crisis on their students. Lisa Ellis, a counselor at a high school in Cleveland, Ohio, developed an eight-week program for first-year students at her school. The program's purpose is to reduce the stigma of mental illness and provide students information on how to get help, if needed. She uses videos such as TED talks focused on mental health, provides information on mental health diagnoses, and teaches ways for students to cope with their emotions. Creation of mental health programs in schools has become a priority amid the growing number of depressive and anxiety-ridden youth.

Inclusiveness

Health professionals, including the US surgeon general, also recommend that schools provide an atmosphere of inclusiveness and acceptance for their students, because this has been found to be a mental health protector for youth. For students to feel connected at school, feeling accepted and respected for who they are—no matter their race, sexuality, or gender—

is essential. Ensuring that young people of all races, genders, sexualities, and ethnicities feel included and supported will lead to better mental health.

Specifically, the CDC and other health organizations support schools implementing inclusive LGBTQ practices, since these youth are less connected to schools, according to 2021 data. CDC studies have found that when schools implement policies and practices that support LGBTQ youth, these actually benefit both LGBTQ students and heterosexual students. Examples of policies that help are using a student's preferred pronouns, establishing gay-straight alliances, and incorporating LGBTQ issues in health classes. These lead to LGBTQ youth feeling more connected to school. The 2021 Trevor Project study found that LGBTQ youth who found their school to be LGBTQ-affirming reported lower rates of attempting suicide. Overall, efforts to increase acceptance are needed to help establish the vulnerable students' connections to school.

Reduce or Establish Better Social Media Use

Mental health professionals also contend that reducing risk factors such as social media use will lead to a healthier mental state for America's young people. Because social media use is tied to peer pressure, comparison to others, and cyberbullying—all of which can lead to anxiety and depression—experts recommend that young people spend less time on social media.

Toward this end, some states are considering laws that limit youth access to social media. One of the strictest social media regulations was enacted in Utah in 2023. The state's new law, which takes effect in 2024, prohibits youth under age eighteen from using social media from 10:30 p.m. to 6:30 a.m., requires age verification for anyone who wants to use social media in the state, and requires parental permission for youth to sign up for sites such as Instagram and TikTok. The difficulty of enforcing laws like this one remains to be seen.

In the meantime, other states, such as Texas and California, are also considering or enacting laws aimed at limiting youth social media usage and ensuring that parents have greater ability to control their children's online presence.

Illustrating the positive effects of decreasing, or even giving up, social media is the experience of a young woman named Aygul. As a college student during the pandemic, Aygul decided to completely give up social media because she realized it was adding to her social anxiety. She felt that constantly checking social media was keeping her away from contact with actual people. The more she engaged on social media, the harder she found it to disengage and interact with people directly. In 2020 she decided to disengage from social media, and since then she has grown into a much more fulfilled, emotionally secure person. "I am happy to say . . . my social anxiety went away. It was a continuous process of healing . . . and now I am a completely, fully functioning individual."[33] She notes that she is now a salesperson, meeting new people every day, and is a much happier, more positive person.

Many believe that if preteens and teens were restricted in their social media use, they might avoid some of the added anxiety that comes with social media usage. As a result, more states are in the process of creating bills to limit youth access.

Sharing Experiences

Aygul shares her story about social media with others to help them understand what she went through. Sharing experiences with others is a way to acknowledge a problem, recognize the feelings that come with that problem, and then find ways to make changes. For these reasons, Julia Paxton has also publicly shared her experiences.

Paxton, of Ohio, graduated with a bachelor's degree in social work in 2021 and is now working as a counselor, wanting to

help young people like herself. She is also a patient advocate for Nationwide Children's Hospital, which helped her as a teen when she struggled with anxiety. In 2017, her senior year of high school, she reached a critical point and was diagnosed with depression. "I was hospitalized a couple of times for suicidal ideation and received treatment for months after that," Paxton writes. "Therapy has saved my life countless times and I now am living in remission and freedom."[34]

Because of the benefits that treatment had for her, Paxton has since been an advocate for mental health awareness and getting rid of the stigma many associate with needing help. She has appeared on *The Today Show*, several podcasts, and interviews to get the word out to youth that reaching out for help is a way to take control of their lives.

Peers Helping Peers

Young people are also helping others by springing into action if they notice a mental health event occurring. In the spring of 2022, teen Jamie Gorman experienced a panic attack while at a New Jersey mall with friends. Gorman felt overwhelmed, dizzy, and short of breath. Because of what they had learned at school, her friends recognized what was happening to her and helped her through it. "They immediately called my dad so he could talk to me. They found a water bottle for me. They sat with me; they were just there for me,"[35] she says. She and her friends had taken part in a program called Teen Mental Health First Aid, offered to students in their school district. The program teaches students how to recognize signs of a mental health crisis and what to do. The students are not trained as counselors. Rather, they learn how to give "first aid" for mental health.

Young people are also staffing hotlines to help other teens in crisis. Oregon, a state that ranks among the worst for youth mental illness and ability to access care, is implementing a variety of programs to help improve the situation. At YouthLine, a crisis line in Portland for struggling teens, teenagers answer the calls of their peers and offer whatever help is needed. In 2013 YouthLine received roughly fourteen hundred contacts. By 2021 it had received twenty-five thousand annual contacts from all across the country.

The teens at the center take calls and texts ranging from how to handle relationship or friendship issues to more serious cases like self-harm or suicide. All of the teen volunteers receive more than sixty hours of training, and supervisors are on standby in the room. Aditi, one of the volunteers, has dealt with depression and received much help from therapy and medication. Now she likes helping others and feels that her experience adds to her ability to relate. "Even if it's just that tiny push or pull that someone needs—off the ledge, and it can be that for one person, then we have done what we need to do," says Aditi. "After

I'm done with YouthLine, if I can go like, yes, I was able to help one person from committing suicide, that's, like, all I need for the rest of my life."[36] Aditi and other young hotline workers feel that their own experiences and age add to their ability to help their peers.

Rising numbers of young people are being proactive in taking care of each other. With the mental health crisis among youth, more action is needed. Making a positive change in young people's emotional health requires continued action, from youth themselves to the government, in order to increase awareness and access to mental health care and reduce the stigma associated with it.

SOURCE NOTES

Introduction: Emerging Crisis

1. Quoted in Matt Richtel, "'It's Life or Death': The Mental Health Crisis Among U.S. Teens," *New York Times*, April 23, 2022. www.nytimes.com.
2. Quoted in Cleveland Clinic, "The Teen Mental Health Crisis: What Adults Can Do to Help," October 3, 2022. https://health.clevelandclinic.org.
3. Quoted in Sandra Westfall, "Inside One Teen Girl's Struggle to Manage Anxiety During the Pandemic," *People*, July 2, 2020. https://people.com.

Chapter One: Teens in Distress

4. Madison Jo Sieminski, "Open Doors," Anxiety & Depression Association of America, February 25, 2020. https://adaa.org.
5. Richtel, "'It's Life or Death.'"
6. Kyle Mitchell, "My Three Steps: How I Went from Socially Anxious to Socially Confident," Anxiety & Depression Association of America, January 6, 2023. https://adaa.org.
7. Manvi Tiwari, "You're the Real Badass," Anxiety & Depression Association of America, May 19, 2021. https://adaa.org.
8. Quoted in Amrita Priya, "Manvi Tiwari: Turning Lived Experiences of OCD and Anxiety into Survival Strategies for People with Mental Health Issues," Global Indian, March 8, 2023. www.globalindian.com.
9. Quoted in Ethan Kee, "What Depression Really Feels Like from Those Who Know," Psychreg, November 26, 2021. www.psychreg.org.
10. Cora Berry, *Depression and Suicide, My Story*, YouTube, 2020. www.youtube.com/watch?v=Nbyt-7udjmg.
11. Quoted in Samantha Gluck, "Teen Shares Self-Injury Secret," HealthyPlace, March 25, 2022. www.healthyplace.com.
12. Quoted in Gluck, "Teen Shares Self-Injury Secret."
13. Waylon Griswold, "Lighting the Way for Others: Hope and Life Renewed," Anxiety & Depression Association of America, June 30, 2022. https://adaa.org.
14. Griswold, "Lighting the Way for Others."

Chapter Two: Causes of the Crisis

15. Quoted in *PBS NewsHour*, *How the Pandemic Is Impacting College Students' Mental Health*, YouTube, January 19, 2021. www.youtube.com/watch?v=4QB00M0cVDE.
16. Quoted in Eduardo Medina, "How Young People's Social Anxiety Has Worsened in the Pandemic," *New York Times,* September 27, 2021. www.nytimes.com.
17. Quoted in Cyberbullying Research Center, "Share Your Cyberbullying Story." https://cyberbullying.org/stories.
18. Quoted in Will McDuffie, "13-Year-Old Indiana Boy Dies by Suicide, Family Says He Was Bullied," ABC News, March 10, 2023. https://abcnews.go.com.
19. Quoted in *60 Minutes*, *Meet the Teens Lobbying to Regulate Social Media*, YouTube, December 11, 2022. www.youtube.com/watch?v=XvM8hqoHXkl.
20. Liz Sanders, "Surviving Trauma, My Story, Part 1," *Consciously Transforming Blog*. www.lizsandersstudio.com.
21. Quoted in Sofia Quaglia, "Study Identifies the Genes That Increase Your Risk of Depression," Verywell Health, June 16, 2021. www.verywellhealth.com.

Chapter Three: Most Vulnerable Youth

22. Quoted in Ariel Zilber, "'I Think It Was Just Words, but Words Hurt': Parents Mourn Death of 12-Year-Old 'Peaceful Soul' Son Who Killed Himself After Bullies Said He Was 'Going to Hell for Being Gay,'" *Daily Mail* (London), December 7, 2021. www.dailymail.co.uk.
23. Quoted in Zilber, "'I Think It Was Just Words, but Words Hurt.'"
24. Quoted in *Frontline*, "Growing Up Trans," PBS, 2021. www.pbs.org.
25. Quoted in Centers for Disease Control and Prevention, "New CDC Data Illuminate Youth Mental Health Threats During the COVID-19 Pandemic," March 31, 2022. www.cdc.gov.
26. Ky, "I Was a Junior in High School," Colorado State University, 2022. wgac.colostate.edu.
27. Quoted in Jessica Bursztynsky and Lauren Feiner, "Facebook Documents Show How Toxic Instagram Is for Teens, *Wall Street Journal* Reports," CNBC, September 14, 2021. www.cnbc.com.
28. Quoted in Christina Caron, "Why Are More Black Kids Suicidal? A Search for Answers," *New York Times*, November 18, 2021. www.nytimes.com.
29. Quoted in Carolyn Jones, "Black Youth Face Rising Rates of Depression, Anxiety, Suicide," EdSource, January 25, 2022. https://edsource.org.

30. Quoted in Jones, "Black Youth Face Rising Rates of Depression, Anxiety, Suicide."

Chapter Four: What Can Be Done to Ease the Teen Mental Health Crisis?

31. Vivek H. Murthy, "Introduction from the Surgeon General," National Library of Medicine, 2021. www.ncbi.nlm.nih.gov.
32. Emma F., "Reaching Out to My Guidance Counselor Saved My Life," To Write Love on Her Arms, February 23, 2021. https://twloha.com.
33. Maggenlove, *I Quit Social Media 2 Years Ago. Here's How My Life Changed—Social Anxiety, Losing Friends & More*, YouTube, 2022. www.youtube.com/watch?v=ozKnEQ6Gipk.
34. Quoted in IN5, "Children's Mental Health Advocate, Julia Paxton, Takes Over Our Insta." https://1n5.org.
35. Quoted in Anya Kamenetz, "A Novel Program for Teens in Mental Health Crisis," *Washington Post*, March 3, 2023. www.washington post.com.
36. Quoted in PBS, "Teen Volunteers Staff Crisis Support Line to Help Peers Facing Mental Health Challenges," January 25, 2023. www .pbs.org.

GETTING HELP AND INFORMATION

Books

Sara Rose Cavanaugh, *Mind over Monsters: Supporting Youth Mental Health with Compassionate Challenge*. Boston: Beacon Press, 2023.

Elizabeth Cronin, *Mindfulness Journal for Mental Health: Prompts and Practices to Improve Your Well-Being*. Emeryville, CA: Rockbridge, 2022.

B. Heidi Ellis et al., *Mental Health Practice with Immigrant and Refugee Youth: A Socioecological Framework*. Washington, DC: American Psychological Association, 2019.

Katie Hurley, *The Depression Workbook for Teens: Tools to Improve Your Mood, Build Self-Esteem, and Stay Motivated*. San Antonio, TX: Althea, 2019.

Charlotte Markey, *The Body Image Book for Girls: Love Yourself and Grow Up Fearless*. Cambridge: Cambridge University Press, 2020.

Internet Sources

American Psychological Association, "Speaking of Psychology: What's Behind the Crisis in Teen Mental Health? With Kathleen Ethier, PhD," 2023. www.apa.org.

Beth Reese Cravey, "Time to Talk About It: Talkable Communities Offers Courses to Spot Youth Mental Health Crises," *Florida Times-Union* (Jacksonville), March 28, 2023. www.jacksonville .com.

Carolyn Jones, "Black Youth Face Rising Rates of Depression, Anxiety, Suicide," EdSource, January 25, 2022. https://edsource .org.

Rasheek Tabassum Mujib, "'You're Not Alone.' Cape High School Students Share Experiences with Suicide," Yahoo!, April 1, 2023. https://news.yahoo.com.

Mitchell Prinstein, "US Youth Are in a Mental Health Crisis—We Must Invest in Their Care," American Psychological Association, January 28, 2022. www.apa.org.

Jean Twenge, "Teens Girls Are Facing a Mental Health Epidemic. We're Doing Nothing About It," *Time*, February 14, 2023. https://time.com.

Websites

Centers for Disease Control and Prevention (CDC)
www.cdc.gov
The CDC is a US government agency that conducts and provides health-related studies, recommendations, and information. Its website provides information on mental health, the teen mental health crisis, and recommendations to combat this crisis.

Mental Health America
www.mhanational.org
This organization is a nonprofit dedicated to promoting mental health and preventing mental illness by its efforts in research, advocacy, education, and awareness. Its website has a specific section focused on the mental health of youth, including information on the signs of mental health issues, specific health conditions, and what people can do for help.

Mental Health Literacy
https://mentalhealthliteracy.org
Mental Health Literacy is an organization dedicated to distributing mental health literacy information, research, education, and resources. Its website provides educational materials on mental health coping strategies, dealing with stress, and staying connected to others.

National Alliance on Mental Illness (NAMI)
https://nami.org
NAMI provides advocacy, education, support, and public awareness to help those with mental illness and their families. This website has a section for kids, teens, and young adults. It addresses how to deal with social media, how to talk to parents and friends if you are experiencing mental health issues, and how to find help.

988 Suicide & Crisis Lifeline

https://988lifeline.org

The 988 Suicide & Crisis Lifeline is a national network of crisis centers that provides support to people in crisis. It operates twenty-four hours a day, seven days a week. Its website provides information on suicide prevention, risk factors and symptoms, and stories of hope and recovery. If you or someone you know is experiencing emotional distress or thoughts of suicide, call 988 for help.

Office of the Surgeon General

www.surgeongeneral.gov

The Office of the Surgeon General provides scientific information on how people in the United States can improve their health. Its website provides youth mental health crisis studies, statistics, and recommendations on what can be done to improve outcomes.

INDEX

PICTURE CREDITS

ABOUT THE AUTHOR

Leanne K. Currie-McGhee lives in Norfolk, Virginia, with her husband, Keith, children, Grace and Sol, and dog, Delilah. She has written educational books for over two decades and is thankful for the opportunity to learn and share.